A

PRECIOUS MOMENTS

CHRISTMAS

GIVEN TO

ON THIS DATE

BY

A

PRECIOUS® MOMENTS

CHRISTMAS

SAM BUTCHER

Tommy
NELSON™

Thomas Nelson, Inc.
Nashville

Scripture quotations are from
The International Children's Bible, New Century Version,
Copyright © 1986, 1988 by Word Publishing.
Used by permission.

Library of Congress Cataloging-in-Publication Data

Butcher, Samuel J. (Samuel John), 1939-
   A Precious Moments Christmas / Sam Butcher.
       p.   cm.
   Summary: Uses rhyme and illustrations to express the thoughts and
feelings of a traditional Christmas.
   ISBN 0-8499-1517-1 (hardbound)
   1. Christmas—Juvenile literature.   2. Precious Moments, Inc.—Juvenile
literature. [1. Christmas.] I. Title.
GT4985.5.B87 1997
394.2663—dc21   97-22769
                                                   CIP
                                                   AC

Printed in the United States of America.

97 98 99 00 01 02 RRD 9 8 7 6 5 4 3 2 1

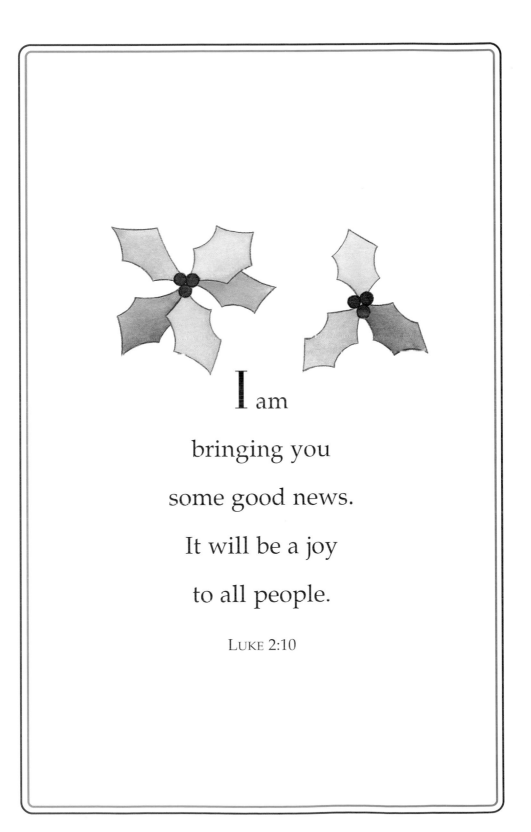

I am

bringing you

some good news.

It will be a joy

to all people.

LUKE 2:10

Christmas is a time

for bows

and jingle bells

and winter snows...

Of holly wreaths

and colored lights

that twinkle in

the snowy nights.

Christmas is

a time for cakes

and other things

that Mommy makes…

Of little stockings

on the wall

with tiny treasures

in them all.

Christmas is

a time of joy

for every little

girl and boy…

A time of toys

and balls and bats

and puppy dogs

and baseball hats.

But just remember

Christmas brings

much more than toys

and other things...

More than tinsel,

more than lights,

more than jingle bells

and snowy nights.

Most of all,

this time of year...

with all its love

and Christmas cheer...

Reminds us of

the gift of love

that came to us

from up above.

For long ago

in Bethlehem

a star arose

above the land.

Little angels
came to earth
to sing the news
of Jesus' birth.

The shepherds heard

their song of joy

and went to see

the baby boy.

Wise men saw

his wondrous star

and made their journey

from afar.

They brought him gifts

of spice and gold

that light-filled day

so long foretold.

Now Christmas is

a time to share

the love of Jesus

everywhere.

A time when we
can laugh and sing
and thank the Lord
for everything.

So when you think

of snowy nights

with sleigh bells, trees,

and Christmas lights…

Above all else

remember, too,

God sent his gift

of love for you.

Merry Christmas!

God Bless You.

Give glory to God in heaven,

and on earth let there be peace

to the people who please God.

LUKE 2:14